WOW! Anthology

Winners and shortlist in Poetry and Fiction
from the
2014 WOW! Awards

First published in 2014 by
Wordsonthestreet
Six San Antonio Park,
Salthill,
Galway, Ireland.
web: www.wordsonthestreet.com
email: publisher@wordsonthestreet.com

ISBN   978-1-907017-32-2

Cover design, layout and typesetting: Wordsonthestreet

Printed and bound in the UK

CONTENTS

POETRY

FICTION

POETRY

WHY I CHOSE THEM
POETRY JUDGE KNUTE SKINNER

Judges often mention that making their final decisions has been difficult and also that, of course, someone else might well have come up with different choices. I can identify with both statements, but, that said, I also feel confident that the poems I've selected are worthy. Here then, are some reasons for my selections.

WOW! 1: I admire the ease with which *Upstream, the Bliss of Heaven* opens with the grim detail of a severed head, passes over just enough river imagery to set the scene, and moves on to the learned allusions of paragraph four – while all the time maintaining an evenness of tone and a focus on the loving relationship of Margaret and her father Thomas More. Is there a word out of place? I don't think so. And the Latin conclusion seems just right.

WOW! 2: *Brent Geese Gathering* has an admirable use of imagery that renders the speaker's relationship with the geese memorable. Moreover, the images manage to contrast the calmness of the geese with their sudden bursts of activity. Language and structure are apt, and I also like the way the poem focuses on the behaviour of these transient geese while also making the narrator meaningful.

The Runners Up: The following poems, listed in no planned order, offer a consistency of quality with a variety of subject matter and treatment.

Reasons to Tend the Front Garden makes good use of anaphora, in this case the frequent repetition of *Because* at the beginning of a number of lines. It also successfully employs rather simple statement, a quality which is often difficult to sustain. It's not *all* simple statement, however. There is vivid imagery and an arresting generalisation. And the implied self-portrait of the narrator works well.

The Riddle of the Artist differs from the other poems selected in that it makes good use of a formal structure: three five-line stanzas in iambic metre. It also makes occasional but effective use of the repetition of the end words *leaves*, *head* and *corn*. Unlike the others, this poem creates an intriguing riddle – the surprising conclusion in which the artist sees his work as his own self.

The Traveller's Tale succeeds largely because of the depictions of the narrator's home town. They are established through brief but vivid recollections of shopkeepers, whose activities suggest a vanishing way of life. In addition, the speaker's relationship to her father – and to herself – is subtly shown.

Puffball is a *tour-de-force* of description, in which images of woodland trees and undergrowth undergo change as the seasons progress. Lovely visual, tactile and olfactory details abound.

Courting is a satirical poem using the fate of Anne Boleyn as a springboard to a discussion of human cruelty, touching on beheadings and witch-drownings and progressing to the present day, represented by the tortures at Guantanamo. The unsettling addresses to the poem's audience provides a strong conclusion.

Finally, in all of these, the runners-up as well as the winners, the poets have shown an assured control of line.

Knute Skinner was born in St. Louis, Missouri, and now lives in Co. Clare, Ireland. His collection, *Fifty Years: Poems 1957-2007*, from Salmon, contains new work along with work taken from thirteen previous books. *The Other Shoe* won the 2004-2005 Pavement Saw Chapbook Award. A limited edition of his poems, translated into Italian by Roberto Nassi, was published by Damocle Edizioni, Chioggia, Italy, in 2011. A memoir, *Help Me to a Getaway*, was published by Salmon in March 2010. A new book of poems, *Concerned Attentions*, was published by Salmon in September 2013. www.knuteskinner.com.

UPSTREAM, THE BLISS OF HEAVEN

KAREN J. MCDONNELL

WOW! 1 Award

Remember that we may, in conclusion, meet with you,
my own dear father, in the bliss of heaven.
– Margaret Roper's letter to Thomas More before his execution.

At dawn Margaret carries home a grisly jewel:
her father's head, retrieved from London Bridge
at no small danger to herself.
She will keep it by her. Always.

August dew is sparking at the river's edge.
Ravens fly into the day. The ghost
of Thomas More sits beside his daughter
and sighs, 'Farewell to fond company.'

Oars plash upstream on the eternal Thames
on a tide of Aesop's fables, the Latin Vulgate,
Astronomy and Rhetoric, *Avé*s and *Te Deum*s.

Margaret shivers, and draws her mantle close.
Thomas whispers in her left ear
'O my Meg, *bona et fidelis filia mea.*'

BRENT GEESE GATHERING

EITHNE CAVANAGH

WOW! 2 Award

Canadians, from Ellesmere Island they come
with a whoosh, to grace our shores
and winter here in family flocks.

Each year I anticipate these Geese
as I would a lover's landing
– the regularity of their arrival
a reassurance that my world is well.

Calmly they graze estuaries
seeking such delicacies
as eelgrass, sea lettuce, tasty algae.
Black necks collared with white feathers
lend an air of Puritan travellers.
Plump bellies boast a lacy pattern.

When suddenly they V-shape
high into the air calling to each other
– a mass of whirring wings – I believe
this aero-show is put on just for me.

In March they gather for the leaving,
their runway a grassy field
or splodgy wasteland.
And then in a gently honking skein they're off.

Wishing them safe journey when they rise
as one great wave, I feel lonely
as if I've lost a treasured loved one
to the skies.

COURTING

AOIFE MANNIX

Anne Boleyn's spaniel tossed from a window
as her ladies snigger behind their hands,
folding into their velvet bodices
tales of incest and gentleman callers.
The slow sipping of poison in wine
as red as blood dares to be while the king
swaps his queen for a pawn. Her neck
carved in glass, her last letter a forgery of love.
His signature neat and tidy for history to read
how he forgot that once he had written God
backwards just to stitch her heart into his own.

In the shadows the peacock wings are stirring,
feather ghosts in the mouth of a condemned man.
Confessions that flutter so softly to the ground
as the sword is sharpened. These public executions
ring through the years of drowning witches,
chemical burnings, the waterboarding
orange silences of Guantanamo towers
where spies record every snowflake.

If you trust in your own innocence
then beware the barking of a small dog
in the night. How the questions spin
and shatter like bones in the mouth
till you are not sure if your children
are your own. The old jealousies,
the old hatred of gypsies, Jews, queers.
If you think it could never happen again,
ask yourself why the king had six wives,
why listen in on so many waves?

These days even the dead
seem capable of betrayal
as a beautiful woman strips
silent as a severed telephone line.

PUFFBALL

ORLAGH O'FARRELL

There was a sudden
yeast of mushrooms in the grass, as if
bread rolls had risen in the night
and next day disappeared.

Slants of sunshine spread through trees
rich with dancing motes.
Conkers, fatter and glossier than before
– you'd stuff your pockets with them.

Cities of honeyfungus springing up
on softened leaf fall
on sturdy trunks and stones.

And how riotous
the reckless trees,
decked out like sweetshops!
Even the thistles put out
tufts of silky fur.

*

Sombre now, the woods are stacked
with stalks and empty seedheads.
Brittle wands bereft, and ghostly purses

hoarding their one last seed.
The dried out thistles are back in drab
snagged with hooks and pins

and all the honeyfungus cities gone
shrunk to a toxic spore.

That tough old Irish ivy
comes thriving up the trees.
Don't you remember its

counter-move, its canny thrift?
Blooming in autumn,
saving in spring.

Its stamens like small boats riding,
anchored through the storm.

Its loamy smell.

REASONS TO TEND THE FRONT GARDEN

SUSAN MILLAR DUMARS

Because it's here.
Because I'm here.
Because it's my house now.

Yellow petals shimmer
like fish scales
after rain.
Dried twig crackle, riddle
of weeds, shrubs skeletal
after a tough winter.

Because the dead must make room
for the living.
Because roots need room to take hold.
Because I love
sun and the shadows of clouds
moving, everything moving,

and I am part of everything.
Because I love
the sweet mourning
in the scent of cut grass.
Because I love.
Because I'm here.

THE RIDDLE OF THE ARTIST

BILL HOAGLAND

I thought to stuff a pair of pants with leaves
and sewed the cuffs and filled a shirt with leaves
to form a chest and arms. I belted these
together with a rope, then shaped a pair
of hands from gloves I fleshed with grass.

I struggled for a way to make a head
and closed my eyes to see what kind of head
imagination might suggest. It said
to stuff a bag with weeds, to paint a pair
of eyes and lips, to shape a nose.

I drove a post between the beans and corn
because raccoon and crow and deer like corn
and beans. I nailed a plank across that post,
then tied my man to stand there rigidly
and stepped aside to see that he was me.

THE TRAVELLER'S TALE

MICHAEL O'CONNOR

Every week he reads my GPS
Coordinates over a crackly phone,
Then tells me how the weather is at home.
He never tells me that he misses me
Or that he hates to be alone.

Every night I dream of the shops in
Old Ballybrack: Murphy's, O'Dwyer's, Miss
Byrne's the chemist ... So far from them in time
And space! This is why I travel: to know
The world as intimately as that place,

And that time when Mr Sheckleton drove
His cattle down the road and left milk in
Glass bottles on our doorstep and the Grays
and Godwins and Murphys and O'Dwyers
Were fixtures in a world as precise as

The metal frame Mr Godwin used to
Distinguish twopenny from fourpenny
wafers while we drank minerals through straws
And gas went up my nose. I remember
It all: how, much later, we bought cigarettes

Singly in Murphy's and shared them leaning
Against the wall outside. Some of us blew
Smoke rings but I could never, then or since.
I eat, I drink, I sleep but cannot rest.
I walk for hours in strange places in search

Of – of something to connect to that's as
Deep and safe and sure as years ago was.
My husband says my children are depressed
And have forgotten me. I think I have
Forgotten me myself, but I remember

Murphy's, and clutching a half-crown in my
Hand for the papers, and the slow walk home,
Chewing a penny bar, avoiding lines
On the pavement. Once, a two shilling piece
Slipped through the boards of a counter as I

Waited to buy sweets. My father rescued
Me and it and calmed my fears. Now I am
That coin, lost in the void. My father's gone.
I'm somewhere in Patagonia and
I may never find myself again.

FICTION

WHY I CHOSE THEM
FICTION JUDGE E.M. REAPY

The WOW! 1 Award goes to *Bodies of Water.* This is a poetic journey, which avoided sentimentality. I enjoyed the alignment of ordinary and extraordinary details. The story unfolds through the Kerry landscape, which is beautifully described. I loved how this flight to England for a termination is paralleled with the GAA match, showing how these trips are also a historic (though unspoken) Irish tradition. The story felt contemporary and political. I thought it was a great vehicle for showing that not all pregnancies terminated are unwanted. Characters and dialogue are natural and one can relate easily to them. The writer has an immediate, unpretentious yet lyrical writing style.

 The WOW! 2 Award goes to *Beneath the Judas Tree.* Despite the title being slightly strained, this story was original, powerful and tragic. At first, I assumed the female character was having an affair and the realisation that she is the mother of a heroin addict came as a shock. It is a compelling hook. Great humanity is shown in the descriptions of the relationships in the piece. Anyone who has been involved with or related to someone with addictions will empathise with this story. Dialogue and pacing are well handled. The violence at the end is terrifying and the scene of the husband and wife crying in the garden at midnight, over their shared loss, is haunting.

 The WOW! Awards runners up:

Foxtails and Soup has very poetic language. Great control and atmosphere are built into the piece. The stifling isolation of family life on a farm is felt throughout. The fox as a metaphor works well within the context of this feud. The writing style is admirably lyrical.

Damage Limitation has an engaging voice. It is humorous at times. Derek as a character is both infuriating and compelling and we can feel Kristin's frustrations as she watches him flounder with his mid-life crisis. It is also an interesting social commentary on casual racism in modern Britain.

The Crown of Snow is atmospheric and I liked that the point of view was with Kate. I loved the suggestion of things with the other characters – the grandfather as a sort of disillusioned poet; the uncle's trips to town; the future for the oldest 'Hooligan' kid who joined the Marines. This is a tenderly drawn piece with a stunning snowy backdrop. I felt the mysteries of the grandfather's past gave it great depth. Kate's desire to break away from this life is something I wondered about long after the story ended. On re-reads, this piece grows in strength.

Housewife of the Year has an experimental narrative structure. The use of scriptwriting language was well handled and worked effectively to show Maisie's desire to escape from her dull life. She reminded me of a sort of murderous Shirley Valentine. It contains some wickedly dark humour and manages to keep the reader sympathetic to the 'Housewife of the Year' despite her ill thoughts and actions.

In *Émigré* the excitement and fear of a young Northern Irish couple as they move to London is captured perfectly. Their building of a home together with limited funds, to their settling in and becoming a family amidst the many millions of people in the big city was very realistic and I was rooting for them to succeed. I loved the hope at the end of the story.

Elizabeth (EM) Reapy is an Irish writer. She has an MA in Creative Writing from Queen's University, Belfast, edits wordlegs.com and is a Pushcart Prize nominee. In 2012, she was Tyrone Guthrie Exchange Writer in Residence to Varuna, Australia and she performed at NYWF in Sydney. She is the director of Shore Writers' Festival in Enniscrone, Co Sligo. In May 2012 she had a no.1 iTunes Literature Podcast with her short story *Getting Better*. She compiled and edited *30 under 30: A Selection of Short Fiction by Thirty Young Irish Writers*. In 2013 she was awarded an Arts Council Literature Bursary and was selected as the Irish representative for PEN International's New Voices Award, where she made the long-list of six writers. She has recently read in Buenos Aires, New York, Listowel Writers' Week and Belfast Book Festival. www.emreapy.com.

BODIES OF WATER

MARCELLA O'CONNOR

WOW! 1 Award

The room closed in. Clodagh lay breathless, twisted around her duvet on the island of her bed. Daylight lined the drawn curtains. She could smell rashers cooking. With this, Mam set the tone for the day. Fry-ups stood for occasions: weddings, funerals, someone returning from America. Now habit would lead them. Clodagh rose. She dislodged two paper shopping bags of still-tagged items from the space in front of her wardrobe, hoping vaguely that someone else would take care of them while she was away. She dug out a clean tracksuit, dressed, tied up her hair. In the kitchen, her parents and brother sat around the table. Clodagh joined them and forced her way through tea and toast. She brushed her teeth in the bathroom then zipped her toothbrush into the suitcase. Mam did the washing up. Donal lingered over his tea. As Clodagh walked out the front door, she overheard Donal instructing Mam to text when they got in.

Clodagh leaned against the car. The damp grass shored up drops of sunlight. Across the road, the neighbours' fields unfolded downhill in neat squares that rolled upwards at the next slope. Beyond that more hills flowed, swelling and falling under the net of stone walls. Distance flattened the sea in the harbour. A lone cloud dragged its shadow over Mount Brandon. She checked her phone. No text. She had hoped for, but not really expected, a text at least. Clodagh still couldn't account for Martin's silence on the phone last night, didn't know if he was angry with her, if he blamed her, or if he just couldn't handle it yet. He said, 'I'll ring you back,' then vanished into the ether. She fretted over whether she had explained it clearly enough.

Mam asked if they had everything before getting into the car. Dad put the suitcase in the boot and took his place behind the wheel. Clodagh drew a last breath of fresh air and sat in. The road carried them away until Ballyferriter lapsed from view.

In Dingle, the bay shone. Páidí the gardener sat on the wall looking posed with boats behind him and light reflected off the water haloing him like a spotlight. Clodagh pulled her hood up. Which was useless. He would know the car. But she wanted the comfort of it. She tugged her hoodie where it rode up on her belly. She didn't know if it hurt. When she thought of it, she felt the same thing as when someone said 'a cutting wind'. That's what it must be like. Each time she remembered, she held herself very still. She hardly moved for as long as town detained them. There, in the thick of red-trimmed pubs and souvenir shops, the usual characters rushed around after their messages. Seán crossed the street with a stack of newspapers. Bridie marched up the footpath with her carrier bags, sending ripples through a line of slow-moving tourists. Clodagh looked out the right-hand window, towards the marina, instead. A boat pulled out. Its engine chopped through the water at low speed like a ticking clock. Coiled rope, plastic crates and piles of green fishing net clotted the parking lot. A boy in a white tracksuit kneeled by a bench. With a pocket knife, he sloughed a shower of silver scales from a fish. Clodagh flinched and looked straight ahead.

After the last roundabout, the road curved upwards through open country, running parallel to a vein of mountain that stemmed from Mount Brandon. Clodagh's eyes absently traced an amputated section of viaduct. Hills obscured the water one moment then revealed slices of bay as the car crawled down hairpin turns. Dad should have gone through Annascaul, but – driven by habit, a phantom trip to the match – turned off for Inch instead. Once he made the turn, neither Clodagh nor Mam could correct him. They would simply persist.

It was hard to lose track of the sea here. Rows of mountain hemmed the road in for a moment. A stone house stood by a stream with white sheets flapping from the line. Ocean appeared again, wedging itself between two hills. The road clung to the side of one of these hills, poised over a vertical drop that made the guard rails look unconvincing. Clodagh told Dad to pull over. He slowed and pulled into a viewing spot on the shoulder. Clodagh got out. She stretched herself into the stillness, breathed in the smell of grass radiating from the fields. The pause lasted as long as she held her breath. She exhaled just as a breeze stirred up the briny smell of sea.

Clodagh crouched. She vomited. Bile coated her teeth. She waited. A clump of sheep fluff on the wire fence ebbed in the wind. Below, deep-set waves rolled towards Inch. Lengthwise, they ran all the way to where the mountains of the Ring of Kerry curled against the horizon. In the intense sun, the mountains were a bright, cloudy blue and so vaporous the sea looked more substantive. Clodagh stood. Her runners gritted over pebbles. Mam handed her a water bottle. She rinsed and spat, got back in the car.

Inch Beach revealed a glimpse of itself before the road dipped downhill and ran flat through the rushes. Dad stopped for cows. Through the open windows, Clodagh could hear hooves on tarmac, creaking ankles, tails swishing at midges. A bee buzzed by her window.

'I should have gone through Annascaul,' said Dad.

Clodagh felt relief that he hadn't. On the left, the Slieve Mish rose like a wall between Inch and Tralee, cutting them off from city and hospital. Mam said traffic would be deadly in Tralee. A boy walking behind the herd clapped the cows off the road and in through a gate. Dad pulled around the last of them.

In Castlemaine, they lost the ocean and the mountains. The distance between houses closed until they were all attached on either side of the road, packed together as if anticipating a town instead of a village. The knot of traffic reinforced this idea as did the sound of kegs unloaded onto the footpath and the panting of an idling truck, but then the buildings thinned out just beyond the shop and fields once again dominated. In Firies, they stopped at a petrol pump outside a house. Clodagh pulled out her phone again. She decided to text Martin, to try and explain. She keyed a few words, backspaced, started again. She erased the new words and then deleted the message altogether. An old man shuffled out with his breakfast plate in hand to take Dad's money.

Leaving Firies, trees grew so thick from the ditch and branches laced so tightly overhead that it was like driving through a green tunnel. They emerged in Farranfore. Dad turned into the airport parking lot, pulled a ticket from the machine, parked. He carried their suitcase inside. No one queued to check in. Not many were flying. They sat in a row of plastic seats. Dad waited with them until the woman at the desk called their flight. Mam and Clodagh offered up their handbags and shoes to the scanner and stepped through the gateway of metal detectors. The ritual felt paltry. Airports anaesthetise a person to the outside world, sterilise away the locality, but bigger airports do this better. Kerry Airport mustered the same atmosphere of

24

anonymity as a bus station. As she and Mam sat down again and waited to board, Clodagh found herself looking over her shoulder for neighbours. She closed her eyes against conversation. In the stretch of nothing, she fought against thinking. Change clanked into a Coke machine. A bottle plunked down. The flap squealed open, reverberated shut. Finally boarding began and she and Mam rose to join the queue.

On the plane, Clodagh checked her phone. She reread the message Martin sent her yesterday morning, the last text before everything went wrong: 'Good luck today. Wish I could be there for you. Let us know how you get on. XXO.' Neither of them could have imagined the appointment being anything other than ordinary. None of them expected it. Mam had been the most matter-of-fact of them all, driving into Tralee with the idea of making a day of it: check-up, lunch, shopping for a few bits and pieces, but after hospital they drove straight home instead. Though she set her jaw with her usual determination to carry on, Mam turned the doctor's vocabulary around in her mouth as if he had hit her with it. 'We must get Donal to look it up on the computer,' she said.

The plane backed away from the gate. Clodagh switched off her phone and thought of the match and how the national anthem would blare through the speakers in Fitzgerald Stadium. The call would resound, gritty with static, over radios and TVs across the county. In barns and kitchens, in dim pubs and stilled shops, the faithful would follow events on the pitch. Clodagh realised that people at the match couldn't conceive of her flying out and she couldn't properly summon up the football atmosphere even though this day served as the backdrop for both. When she returned, she'd lose her place in the liturgy of small talk. The shopkeeper would say, 'That was some match.' And she wouldn't know whether the response should be, 'In fairness, it was close,' or, 'Jesus, Tyrone really are a shower of dirty feckers.' She would have to reply, 'Yeah.'

The engines strained to life. The seatbelt felt cold against her skin. She tugged her hoodie down. The plane bumped to the start of the runway. It paused. The engines whinnied at full power. The plane lurched forward, taxied smoother as it worked itself up to full speed, lifted off. With her hands Clodagh cradled the round of her belly against the surge of gravity. She knew, whatever Martin thought, that she was doing the right thing.

Fields shrank to patched green squares like continents that cracked and would drift. Mountains filled Clodagh's window. She pictured the view at the match. From the terrace, the curve of mountains echoed the curve of stadium like extra large stands, like seats for the gods. Outside the plane window, the mountains were miniature mock-ups of themselves.

Putting distance between herself and yesterday was almost as good as putting time between them. In the air, yesterday was unreal enough to remember properly. The one sensation that stuck with Clodagh was the feeling of the nurse clutching her hand. The doctor had been moving the wand over her belly. He adjusted the angle and scowled at the screen. He hadn't said a word in five minutes when Clodagh asked, 'What's wrong?' The doctor held up a finger, replaced the wand and left the room. He returned with two other doctors. He put the wand on her belly again, scribbled with it until he found the right place, pointed at the screen. Clodagh intercepted the look of shock that passed between the two new doctors. 'What's happening?' The nurse squeezed her hand and said, 'It's OK. Just relax.' More doctors walked into the room to gather around the ultrasound. 'Why won't anyone tell me what's going on?' demanded Clodagh. The first doctor looked at her, troubled, as if surprised to see her still there.

The plane surfaced over a cloud that erased the landscape below. The landing gear retracted with a mechanical whinge. Rare. Congenital. Unviable. The doctor's words marched through Clodagh's mind. In the end, he had left the nurse to translate for him. 'But really,' the nurse added, 'because of the law in Ireland, there's nothing we can do for you. You just have to wait for nature to take its course.'

Over the Irish Sea, the clouds thinned and broke up. The water glittered beneath them. Clodagh breathed out and for a moment let herself feel free.

BENEATH THE JUDAS TREE

SIOBHAN MURTAGH

WOW! 2 Award

Late one July evening, Eleanor is standing in her dining room spooning cream over her husband's raspberries when the phone rings. She sets the dish down and crosses the dark wooden floor into the hall.

'Hello?' she says.

There is no reply.

'Hello?' she says again. 'Hello?'

She waits. No one answers, but she senses someone at the other end. She listens carefully and is almost sure that she can hear a bare rasp of breath. Her heart starts to thump.

'Is that you?' she whispers. 'Is it?'

A faint noise, like the movement of fabric, carries down the line. Then silence. Seconds pass and then there is the click of a receiver and a dial tone. She stands for a moment, the phone heavy in her hand, and then she hangs up. She goes to the front door. Through the glass she can see the garden, its colours muted in the twilight. The street is empty. She watches the pale globes of the hydrangeas tossing about in the soft breeze. She waits for a moment, until her breathing slows, then returns to the dining room and sits.

'Who was it?' asks John.

'Hmm?' she says. 'Oh … wrong number I think.'

She gets up again and walks to the French doors.

'It's so hot in here,' she says, as she pushes them open. A moth flutters by her and lands on the lightshade over the table. The scent of stock wafts in. When she turns into the room she catches John staring at her over the rim of his glasses. He bends his head to his empty bowl.

In the night she lies awake, her mind filling with scenarios that might come to pass, scenes that may play out. She is convinced that it was him on the phone. Her stomach is tight with nerves, or is it fear? Or is it hope? It has been so long since she has seen him. She misses him more as time goes on, not less, as they all suggested. She badly needs to see him, just see him; she wouldn't ask for anything more.

27

The curtain blows silently into the room and is sucked back against the opening as the breeze changes. Despite the open windows, the room is still too warm. She turns over. John is sleeping on his side with his leg out over the sheet. She notices that his face shows its age when it is slack. When awake, his expressions make him look younger. His eyes still crinkle up when he smiles. She loves his smile. She does. Despite everything that has happened, she still loves his smile.

Morning brings some welcome cloud cover, though the air remains heavy. The weatherman says there is a chance of thunderstorms to come. Over breakfast she wonders silently if he will ring again. She is deep in thought when John asks what her plans are for the day.

'Oh – Mr Dawes is coming. We're going to make a start on the end border.'

He kisses her on the head as he leaves.

'Don't work too hard in the heat,' he says over his shoulder on his way out.

She smiles weakly back at him.

By nine o'clock she is down by the shed loading tools into the rusty wheelbarrow. Mr Dawes enters by the side gate and waves. He makes slow progress across the garden to her, pausing to deadhead or pick up a dry leaf as he goes. When he reaches her she sees that already there are beads of sweat on his forehead. He wears heavy slacks and a long-sleeved shirt rolled up to the elbows, whatever the weather. They greet each other and talk about what work they will do that day. There is a Judas tree at the end of the garden that is not doing well. Its leaves are browning and there is dead wood among the branches. An old buddleia is growing too close to it and is drowning out the light. They plan to lift the shrub and mulch the tree with manure.

She likes working alongside Mr Dawes. He says little as they dig and drag the unruly shrub between them. Some butterflies hover above them, trying in vain to land on the swaying purple blooms of the buddleia, disturbed by the havoc that is suddenly upon them. The trunk is tilted and most of the roots are exposed and swinging wildly when she hears the house phone ring.

She takes off her gloves and holds them in one hand as she crosses the lawn. She steels herself from running. As she nears the door the ringing stops. She steps into the kitchen. The house is silent. She imagines that she hears the echo of the last ring bouncing off the walls. Then it rings again. She lurches forward to the hall and grabs the receiver.

'Hello?' she says, breathless now.

The same silence as before.

'Martin? Is that you?'

'Yeah, it's me,' he says. 'I really need to see you.'

The sound of his voice makes her stomach jump. It takes her a second to settle her breath enough to speak.

'Why did you hang up last night?'

'I shouldn't have rung at that time. I forgot he'd be there.'

He tells her that he is nearby, that he can come to see her now.

'No. You can't be in the house. I'll come to you.'

She makes her excuses to Mr Dawes and leaves in her gardening clothes. If she delays he could change his mind and not be there when she arrives. It is a short walk to the waste ground behind the supermarket. She pulls back the torn wire and squeezes through. The ground is uneven and overgrown with tall dock weeds gone to seed. All about there are mangled wheels, tyres, strips of rusting metal. She treads carefully through the debris. The smell of rotting food rises up from some burst refuse sacks, around which a colony of bluebottles is buzzing. She makes her way towards the wall that has been sprayed with the word 'SKELP' in huge red letters. She is happy. Happy to be seeing her son again, even though it is here, even though she does not know what she will find when she sees him.

As she nears the wall she can see a figure through the weeds and the dusty air. She hears the sound of coughing, a wet, dirty cough. Just for a second she wants to turn and walk away, back to Mr Dawes, back to the problem of the tree, which now seems not to be a problem at all. But in a moment, he is in front of her, sitting on the hard ground, his knees drawn up to his chest.

He sees her and stands up. She is shocked – horrified by how thin he is now, by the grey pallor of his face, by the sores that have broken his skin. She holds out her arms and he comes towards her. Although he is a head taller than her, he rests his head on her shoulder. His arms are limp against her back. She can feel his spine through the thin fabric of his T shirt. There is a smell from him not unlike the rubbish smell that she has passed. She wants to cry. She wants to squeeze him hard in her arms and howl but instead she pulls back and smiles up at him.

'It's so good to see you,' she says.

He smiles too and she catches sight of his blackened teeth.

'How have you been?' she asks. 'How are you?' And she means it. She wants to know everything about him, about every detail of his life.

'Not too bad,' he says, and he sits back down.

She hunkers down beside him.

He tells her that he is doing well, that he is clean; that he is going to his meetings and staying away from the bad crowd.

'The problem is … there is an old debt that they are after me to settle.'

He can't break free, he says, while they are after him. He needs money so he can pay them off and really make a new start.

She knows, of course, that it is all lies. She can tell by his deep, wide pupils and the oily sheen on his face that he is still using. She agrees to help him, but only because it means that she will see him again. If she says no, he will walk away and she will be back to the hell of missing him. It is hard, achingly hard, to see him like this, but pain comes in many forms and you must choose the one that you can bear the best. This is what she has learnt from him, her baby boy.

'Back here tomorrow at twelve,' she says.

'*Tomorrow?* But that's too late. I need it tonight. They'll break my legs if I don't have it.'

They arrange to meet that night at the bottom of the garden. She will have the money. He mustn't make a sound, she tells him; he knows how it will end if his father finds out.

The buddleia is gone when she returns. Mr Dawes has dragged it to the compost heap and is sawing it into pieces. She makes tea for them both and they sit to drink it on the bench beside the heady Mock Orange. She notices him glancing at her and wonders if there is something about her that is giving her away.

'This heat makes everyone crazy, doesn't it?' she says. He gets up without answering and returns to his work.

She pulls the bedroom door softly behind her. Out on the landing the heat is a throbbing presence. She pads over to the stairs and grips the bannister, using it to lighten her weight on the creaking boards as she descends. She pauses at the bottom and listens. Not a sound. She moves silently through the hall and kitchen and out onto the patio. The slabs feel cool and moist against her feet. Above her, the sky is without a star. The air is dense with moisture and she feels its pressure against her lungs.

He is already there, hiding behind the Judas tree, kicking at the loose soil that Mr Dawes has forked over. He appears to be shivering and when she gets up close she sees that his eyes are heavy and bloodshot.

'Martin?' she whispers. 'Are you sick?'

He goes to speak but a hacking erupts and he turns away and puts his hand over his mouth. He tries to hold the cough inside, his back bent over, his chest heaving involuntarily. She can hear great amounts of phlegm gurgling in his lungs, making its way into his mouth. He clears his throat and spits the mucus onto the ground. Wiping his hand on his jeans, he turns to her.

'Have you got it?' he asks.

She steps towards him and puts her palm to his forehead. It is burning up as it did during those childhood illnesses: chicken pox, earache, the flu. It is the same burning, the same child.

'Martin. You're not well. You need a doctor.'

He sighs, a deep, exasperated sigh.

'Well? Do you have the money?'

She takes the bundle of notes from the pocket of her robe and hands it to him.

'At least let me help you. You need an antibiotic. That chest won't get–'

'*Three hundred?*' he says, now wide-eyed and alert. 'I said a thousand. That's what I owe them. I told you how much.'

'That's all my machine will give out in one day.'

He strikes his fist against the tree. '*Jesus,*' he says, throwing back his head.

A memory comes to her clear and sharp: Christmas morning, his seventh year. A yellow go-kart on the driveway, Martin red-eyed and furious.

'It's not the one!' he yelled. 'It should be the blue one with the gears.' John had said he would get over it, that he would come to like it eventually; but he never did. Year after year the go-kart sat, barely used, rusting slowly; a reminder of their failure to ensure his happiness. And he was often so – discontented with what they had to offer, and later, with what the world had to offer. As he drifted into adulthood, the opportunities to please him ran out and his disappointment seemed to harden into bitterness and disillusionment.

'You don't understand, Mum … these guys mean business.'

She placates him, soothes him. She understands now. Tomorrow night; she will have the rest by then.

As she sees him out the gate the first fat drops of rain fall. A rumble of thunder unsettles the silence. She feels sick in her stomach, wondering where he will shelter when the lightning comes, worrying about his chest in the damp air.

She sleeps late the next morning and John has left by the time she wakes. Mr Dawes arrives while she is still at breakfast. She watches him through the kitchen window, circling the Judas tree, examining the ground.

She waves hello and leaves immediately for the bank. The sky is clean and the air is fresher since the rain. In town she makes a call to her doctor. Sick, she tells him; a chesty cough. Productive? Indeed it is – green sputum and fever too. Too ill to leave her bed. Imagine – at this time of year. Could he fax a prescription to the chemist? She appreciates it. She will be in soon for her check-up. John? He is well, thanks. No problems at all. John is always well.

That afternoon she prepares a package: the medicine, a tube of ointment, some food and the money. It gives her pleasure, this doing for him. She places it behind the cleaning bottles under the kitchen sink. She remains kneeling there a moment, before the open press. Her arm reaches again for the package. She hesitates. Then she leans in and takes out half the notes. It is soon to say goodbye again, too soon to let him go.

It was John who had put him out of the house. That day when they discovered her engagement ring was gone. 'No more,' he told her. 'We can do no more.'

That evening Martin returned to a black bag of clothes on the step. John braced himself against the door as he tried to force his way in. She'll never forget the power of John's arms, ramrod strong, pushing against the door; keeping her son from her.

'Please,' she cried, 'one more chance.'

But John just shook his head.

Later, when the banging and shouting had stopped, he held her firmly by the shoulders.

'Eleanor. This boy will be the death of you,' he said. 'Let him go.'

Locks were changed, new Sim cards bought, bank accounts closed. And Martin vanished into thin air.

She is waiting at the end of the garden, behind the tree, out of sight of the house. The sky is strewn with a million stars. The moon hangs sharp and full. The garden gives up its fragrances: cut grass, the woody scent of shrubs, the tang of newly laid manure. Way off in the distance two cats are fighting. She waits and waits.

She hears him first; something overturning in the side passage. Then he is there, running across the lawn, silvered by the light, his path erratic. His body is taut, his movements jerky. He is scratching at his bare forearm. He comes under the tree. His eyes are deep black holes, his cheek is twitching madly. He is grimacing, sniffing, tearing at his skin. His lungs rattle and wheeze. She feels a cleaver rip down through her gut. She had forgotten how it was.

'Martin? I've brought you some things.'

'The money? Where is it?' His voice is tight.

She takes it from the bag and hands it to him.

'And look. Tablets for you, and something for those sores.'

He flicks quickly through the wad of notes.

'I don't believe it. Where's the rest?'

'Well … tomorrow. I can …. But look, take these ...'

She holds out the bag to him. And suddenly he strikes out and knocks it from her hand. She staggers back. The soil crumbles underfoot. She stumbles and lands on the damp ground.

He stands above her. He sucks in air through closed teeth.

'I asked you. I asked you. I asked you.'

He is pacing, turning, clenching his fists.

She cannot bear his distress.

'Martin? OK. I can get it.'

'*I asked you*,' he shouts. And suddenly he is beside her, kneeling on the ground, his hands around her neck.

His hands are strong. He presses hard. She can feel the blood filling her head. Her eyes begin to bulge. Pressure. Pain. And then his voice grows quieter. The stars dim out. The smell of earth is close.

Better this way, she thinks. Better to go at his hands than to live on in this way.

She hears another voice loud and near. There is shouting, footsteps. The swoosh of air in her lungs. His hands are gone. The side gate slams. John is beside her. He holds her arms and helps her to sit.

'I knew,' he says. 'All along, I knew.'

For a long moment he looks at her. Brushes a clump of soil from her hair. His fingers caress her neck. He pulls her to him. His head sags forward against her shoulder. His body shudders. He starts to cry, high, anguished cries that she has never heard before; sounds akin to the distant cats. All that pain. She never knew. She reaches up, pauses. Slowly, slowly, she runs her fingers along his face. They sit there, together, beneath the Judas tree.

DAMAGE LIMITATION

ROBERT GROSSMITH

Sometimes when they watch *Newsnight* together Kristin plays a little game with herself: which story will vex Derek the most? The item about MPs on the make, or phone-hacking red-tops, or tax-dodging celebrities? Or perhaps the piece about Premiership footballers with their super-injunctions? Or it might be the kiss-and-tell 'models' gagged by those injunctions. To tell the truth, there's not much on the news these days that doesn't upset Derek. Kristin plays her game more as a way of masking her irritation with her husband, of sublimating her own secondary anger, than for any pleasure she might derive from this act of matrimonial clairvoyance.

Grumpy Old Man doesn't come close. Once upon a time, before she met him, when he was still in the band, Derek was a committed lefty. He used to go on anti-racism rallies, anti-apartheid marches, the band played miners' benefit gigs, Free Nelson Mandela concerts, the whole Red Wedge thing. His sympathies were boundless.

Now that oceanic circle of sympathy has shrunk to a tiny rocky islet, with room for himself and little else besides. Now he seems to hate everyone, regardless of race, colour or creed. Politicians, social workers, farmers, teachers, the police, the clergy, the unions, TV presenters – they all come in for the Derek treatment. He doesn't vote these days because he says that anyone who puts themselves up for public office must by definition be doing so for the pursuit of corrupt personal ends.

He hasn't written a song in years. Sometimes the other members of the band will phone him up and suggest getting together, maybe working on some new material, even trying to arrange a nostalgia tour. He tells them nostalgia ain't what it used to be haha, and anyway he hasn't picked up a guitar since the turn of the century. Which Kristin knows to be untrue actually, because once or twice when she's arrived home from work unexpectedly early she's heard him strumming away in the front room, even crooning softly to himself on one occasion. He stopped the second her key hit the lock.

Derek works part-time at the city library, where he's in charge of the music section and something of a minor celebrity. She still hears some of the old songs on the radio now and then. 'Land of Ire', for example, his anthemic take on the Troubles. Or 'Untied Kingdom' with its pro-devolution stance: 'Whaddya say / Let's go our own way /I'll move out and you can stay / Cos it's been fun but hey.' He never ventured very far for his wordplay or his rhymes.

She persists in thinking of these songs as Derek's, even though he gets nothing in the way of royalties any more, having sold all the rights to the other band members for a ludicrously small sum when he hit rock bottom around century's end. The other week she heard a few bars of 'Damage Limitation' – actually a song about heroin – on a TV ad for car insurance. She didn't tell Derek.

They have no sex life to speak of, and never speak of the sex life they no longer have, though they still share the same bed, more out of habit than from a desire for conjugal intimacy. His guitar isn't the only thing he hasn't strummed in years. It occurs to Kristin that maybe the two things – the creative block and the libidinal slump – are connected.

All along the street there are For Sale and To Let signs jostling for attention. Everywhere the talk is of austerity, cutbacks, economic collapse, the end of the good times. This part of north Norwich was never the most fashionable even during those good times. Now the area seems to have taken a further precipitous dive downmarket, to have given up entirely on its aspirations and become the almost exclusive domain of single mothers, students, immigrants and the disabled, conveniently serviced by nearby Magdalen Street's endless parade of charity shops, discount stores, pawnbrokers and nearly-new outlets. Never mind Untied Kingdom, a walk along Magdalen Street is like a guided tour of Breadline Britain, Broken Britain, Bankrupt Britain, whichever alliterative put-down you prefer.

In late March they get new neighbours, a Muslim couple. Derek watches from behind the front-room curtains as they unload their stuff from a white Transit – it takes several trips – commenting disparagingly on their furniture and other possessions.

'Why d'you have to spy on them like that?' Kristin says. 'Come away from the window, can't you? It's making me nervous.'

'Computer looks ancient,' he says. 'Bulky old monitor. Least we know they're not terrorists or they'd have a much fancier computer than that.'

The Saturday after the new neighbours move in, they have a party. Perhaps party is too grand a word for it because there doesn't seem to be any music and there's only a handful of guests. The trouble is all these guests – all the male ones anyway – seem to be inveterate chain-smokers and choose to do their chain-smoking congregated in the back garden by the open kitchen door, in other words just a few feet below and to the left of Kristin and Derek's bedroom window. The loud incomprehensible babble of conversation is still going on when they turn in around midnight.

'It's fuckin outrageous,' Derek says. 'You wouldn't get British people behaving like that.' A look from Kristin. 'Well, you wouldn't. Common fuckin decency. Why do they have to talk and smoke outside? Why can't they talk and smoke in the kitchen like everyone else does at parties?'

'Go and have a word with them if you feel that strongly,' Kristin suggests, in the absolute certainty that he won't.

'Why should I? Why should I get out of bed and get dressed and ask them ever so politely if they could possibly be a bit quieter if it isn't too much trouble? It should be fuckin obvious they're disturbing us.'

His voice is now on an unstoppable upward ascent, both in volume and emotional intensity. If we can hear them, Kristin thinks, then presumably they can hear us, or rather Derek. Perhaps they think we're having an argument, perhaps they don't even realise Derek's anger is directed at them.

She tries to reason with him, to get him to show some understanding or, failing that, some charity. It's Saturday night. There's no music. They've only just moved in, they're entitled to a small housewarming. 'D'you remember the party we had when we moved here? Probably a lot noisier than theirs. Why don't we sleep in the spare room tonight? It's only for one night.' But none of this cuts any ice.

'Hubba hubba hubba,' Derek is saying in mock imitation of the gruff guttural accents below.

'Well at least we can close the window. That'll keep some of the noise out.'

'Why should we have to close the fuckin window? You know I can't sleep with the window closed. Especially on a night like this.'

It's true, he always likes to have the window open, even in winter. And tonight is one of the muggiest nights of this record-breaking early spring. The torpid air feels like an extra blanket.

But apparently he changes his mind about the window because suddenly he switches on the bedside lamp, casts aside the single sheet they're lying under and jack-knifes out of bed, stark naked. He flings the curtains apart and, for the space of a couple of seconds while he presses down on the stubborn sash window and noisily bangs it shut, he's fully exposed in his nakedness to the little huddle of people below. Kristin cringes and ducks her head under the sheet as if to obliterate the image. She prays there are no women – no Muslim women – down there.

Closing the window doesn't make much difference, nor apparently does Derek's display of literally naked aggression. The chattering goes on unabated, though muted somewhat by the double glazing. Around one o'clock Derek really begins to hit his stride.

'This is fuckin unbelievable,' he's saying. 'The fuckers. The fuckin fuckers.'

The next thing she knows he's on his feet again, flinging the curtains wide open, lifting the window up and leaning out to scream into the darkness below.

'Shut the fuck up, will you? You've got a whole fuckin house there. Why don't you go inside and discuss your fuckin suicide-bomber plans there?'

With that he slams the window shut again, yanks the curtains together and falls back into bed. 'Let them put that in their fuckin hubbly-bubbly and smoke it.'

Some moments later she hears the noise drop to nothing and the kitchen door click closed.

On the Monday evening there's a knock at the front door. Two uniformed police officers, squad car conspicuously parked outside. They ask Kristin to confirm that Derek lives there and is at home. They'd like to speak to him. He's in the shower. They'll wait.

38

'The police? What do they want?' he shouts above the roar of the water.

'I've no idea, I didn't ask. I assumed you'd know what it was about.'

It turns out it's about his behaviour on Saturday night.

'We've had a complaint that you exposed yourself at the window and shouted racial abuse,' the older-looking of the policemen says.

'And that's a crime, is it?' Derek asks in a misguided attempt at humour, but the policemen don't respond, just wait for a proper answer.

He tries to explain. Hot night. Lot of noise. Couldn't sleep. Early hours of the morning.

'I didn't expose myself. I didn't even know they could see that part of me. I just stood at the window and asked them if they could keep the noise down.'

'You asked them if they could keep the noise down?' the older copper repeats dubiously.

'Well, told them. Told them to keep the noise down.'

The copper consults his notebook. 'You didn't say, Why don't you make your effing suicide-bomber plans indoors?'

Derek sighs as if the copper is splitting hairs. 'Well, I may have done, I suppose, I don't remember. It was two o'clock in the morning.'

One o'clock, Kristin thinks. It was one o'clock.

'Can I suggest, sir,' the younger copper says, 'if you have any problems with noisy neighbours in the future' – he pronounces it *footure*, the Norfolk way – 'you let your wife have a quiet word with them instead.'

It's the holiday Monday of the long Diamond Jubilee weekend and Kristin is in a foul mood. She's volunteered her services – and Derek's too – at the street party under the flyover in Magdalen Street and now she's regretting it. The weekend's been a complete washout so far and the forecast for today is little better. Kristin feels sorry for the Queen: a rain-lashed barge trip down the Thames followed by a raucous concert outside her front gates. If Derek had been married to the Queen, he'd have complained about the noise.

In the event the weather forecast is wrong and it stays fine for most of the day, and anyway the large flapping awning above the barbecue that Kristin and Derek are deputed to supervise shelters them from all but the worst of the cold, slanting rain. At one of the tables underneath the flyover their burqa-clad neighbour sits alongside another Muslim woman and a gaggle of small children, resplendent in their feast-day finery.

Derek points the little group out to Kristin. 'Don't imagine they'll be availing themselves of our prime British beefburgers,' he says. 'Not halal, of course,' he adds unnecessarily. 'Still, dressed like that, least they won't get wet.'

Kristin grits her teeth and says nothing.

But Derek isn't finished. 'Interesting to note the lack of husbands, though. What does that tell you about their attitude to this country?'

She snaps, she can't help it. 'Shut the fuck up, will you?' she hisses.

Heads turn in their direction. Derek stands with his mouth agape. He isn't used to this kind of language from Kristin, he isn't used to this kind of Kristin.

'What?' he says. 'What?'

She waits till the heads have turned away, though she knows people are still listening. Frankly, she doesn't care. But she lowers her voice anyway. 'I'm so sick of this. Sick of you. These constant snide comments, I've had enough, Derek. You've turned into a small-minded, small-town bigot.'

Derek says nothing, just wipes his hands on his striped butcher's apron, then returns to flipping burgers. 'Well. Nothing like telling it like it is,' he says finally.

Later that evening, back home, there's an unbearable tension between them that demands to be addressed. What she'd like to say is that sometimes she feels she's been hoodwinked, as if the man she fell in love with has been incrementally stolen over the years and replaced with another man she doesn't much like. But what she actually says is somewhat more appeasing in tone.

'You've changed so much, Derek, I barely recognise you sometimes. All you do is complain. You've become so bitter, so cynical and jaundiced. You automatically think the worst of everyone, you never give anyone a chance. What's happened to you? You didn't use to be so mean-spirited. What happened to your youthful idealism?'

He lets out a short, barking laugh. 'Hah! My youthful idealism. Yeah, what did happen to that? I'll tell you what happened to it. Life, that's what happened to it. Reality, that's what happened to it.'

'And this is how you intend to carry on, is it? Despising everyone and everything, because ...'

She stops herself just in time.

'Because what?'

She pauses, a long thoughtful pause, before delivering the sentence that waits fully formed in her head, a sentence she knows may herald the end of their life together. 'Because I don't know if I want to carry on being married to someone who hates the human race.'

And it's true, she really doesn't know. Some days she thinks Derek's bilious view of the world is a small enough price to pay for the kind of settled, comfortable life she leads. And other days she resolves to tell him she's leaving. With no kids to factor into the equation – a treacherous subject she ought perhaps to avoid, given that the tests clearly established that their difficulties in conceiving weren't down to her – it could be a clean break, or as clean as it gets. Who knows, this could be the best thing for both of them.

But every time, when the fateful moment approaches, she wavers and falters, she puts it off: I'll wait another day, one more day won't make much difference. And so it goes on, one more day followed by one more day. Eventually, she knows, if she doesn't act soon, all those days will add up to a lifetime.

In July their Muslim neighbours move out and soon afterwards a young Japanese couple take their place – students, Kristin guesses, judging by their age and clothes, namely black leather jackets and T-shirts. Or is she guilty of stereotyping too, just like Derek?

To be fair, he has managed to modify his behaviour somewhat since Kristin's outburst on Jubilee weekend. He doesn't verbally abuse the TV quite as much as he used to, contenting himself instead with a weary sigh and a headmasterly shake of the head. He rations his vitriol.

One day in late summer Kristin comes home early following a computer crash at work and is surprised to hear the sound of singing and guitar-playing, Derek's singing and guitar-playing, coming from the back garden. She steps onto the tiny patio and there he is, at the little wooden table with one of his guitars on his lap. And opposite him, dressed all in black and flashing dazzling smiles in her direction, are their new Japanese neighbours.

'Hi, sweetheart,' he says. 'This is Yuki and Aki. Guess what? They're big fans of my stuff.'

The boy – would that be Yuki or Aki? – smiles even more broadly. 'Big fans,' he says.

'*Big* fans,' the girl repeats with emphasis.

'It's amazing, they've got all our albums. Even a rare bootleg I didn't know existed. I was sitting here working on a new arrangement of 'Untied Kingdom' when I heard them joining in with the words from over the fence. They didn't believe me at first when I told them who I was.'

'Didn't believe him,' the girl repeats, and hides her laughing face in her hands.

Kristin brings everyone glasses of beer – non-alcoholic for Derek, of course – and sits and chats for a while. It turns out they're studying design at the College of Art. Sometimes they lapse into excited Japanese with each other, as if they're already memorialising the present moment for future reference, something to put in a tweet for their friends back home.

After they leave, Derek's in an expansive mood. She hasn't seen him looking this pleased with himself in years. 'Can you believe it? They knew all the words. After all this time! In Japan! Nice couple, I've invited them over for dinner at the weekend.'

Somehow she would have preferred it if he'd been less welcoming to their new neighbours, if he'd given Kristin a lecture instead about illegal whaling operations or nuclear accidents or currency manipulation, at least that would have been true to type. The idea that simple vanity and self-regard could neutralise his xenophobia, could magically transform him from carping misanthrope into Mr Nice Guy, is a deeply unsettling one, and it's enough in the end to tip the scales.

That night they make love – earnestly but tenderly, and for Kristin regretfully – and the following morning she tells him she's leaving.

ÉMIGRÉ

JULIA RODDY

The sky was a pale October nameless grey and it felt like it was closing in on us, reclaiming us. Will locked the car, relieved we had made it this far. We walked to the little red and green cabin door and stepped outside. The wind pulled us back and we laughed at the irony of its force, as if it was begging us to stay. Hand in hand the certainty in our feet stepped forward with a conviction that something better awaited us. We didn't look at each other; we kept our heads tucked into our chins to avoid the cold, sharp attack of rain pelting at us. We climbed the steel ladder up onto the top deck and clung to the steel railings as we walked to the back of the boat to bid our farewell to the country that had nurtured us, through troubled times. I already felt nauseous and we hadn't moved an inch. We stood huddled together on the boat for Scotland and then on to London. 'A whole new world,' my mother Annie had said with gritted teeth. 'It's all ahead of you, Ella,' said Nana encouragingly. We were silenced by the enormity of what we were leaving behind us. I held on to the little relics in my pocket that Nana had given me before leaving. I had forgotten who the saints were, I had accepted the relics disbelievingly but I knew they were for protection, and I needed them now. I kept seeing Annie fighting the tears and I wondered why it took her so long to show me she cared. All those years I questioned the icy distance as if I carried some kind of threat. Will put his forehead onto mine and held me in his warmth. 'I'll put our stuff into the cabin,' he said. I stood up on the top deck watching the pier awash with activity; muscular, windswept faces of men lifted ropes and ladders. Police and army drifted about with walkie-talkies, surveillance helicopters flew overhead, horns blew, whistles screamed, people smiled and waved goodbye, some joked because they were beginning something new, but I saw others, just like us, with bewilderment spread across their faces, people with stories to tell. Will returned with a bottle of water for me, smiling. We stood and watched the boat pull away into a fog. Larne disappeared so quickly we didn't have time to question any of it. Will wrapped me in his arms and I could feel his heartbeat on my back. Finally, three hearts beat together as one. Eventually I fought the nausea and slept beside my lover. I awoke to the sound of the engines rumbling and loud horns. Will was standing over me with anticipation. I got up and we went outside to watch our arrival, a rainbow stretched across a clear blue sky. We were safe. We were free. There was no looking back and it didn't matter who was Catholic or who was Protestant.

We drove to London in my fully packed red Renault four car listening to Prefab Sprout and Santana over and over. We finally arrived into the bright lights of London at ten o'clock that night. It was so full of promise, people dressed in their finery, people with different skin colours to our opaque Irish white. There were shops and restaurants everywhere – Indian, Thai, whatever your desire – zoomed-up cars with hoods down and music blaring. Luke met us at Piccadilly station and we followed him to his home in Maida Vale. He opened the door to his flat with the same excitement I remember him having the day our parents left us to go and visit the Pope. When we stepped inside he hugged me with gusto and Will put out his hand politely, and with a hint of caution Luke grabbed it and pulled him in for a hug too. London had made him a man, and a happy one it, seemed. We still had our coats on when he brought us in to meet his girlfriend Petra, who was sitting on the edge of the sofa shyly; a beautiful looking Indian girl dressed in a sari stood up and bowed her head at us as if we were royalty and then she opened her mouth and spoke with a thick English, quirky, accent. She had made us a pot of hot pumpkin soup and she laughed later as she told us how Luke had bribed her into wearing a sari. We slipped into our new world without a hindrance.

Two weeks later we got up at five a.m. on a Monday morning to start our separate journeys into work. Will had secured a job in a youth centre, a place he described as something akin to a mental institution. For me it was a maze of chaotic tube stations shoulder to shoulder with strangers. My first job was in St Teresa's hospital, as an assistant psychologist to a group of old-hand doctors who were mostly set in their ways. Basically I did the paperwork and administration, and occasionally through Cecilia I got to do a case study when they were oversubscribed. Cecilia was a typical Londoner, with an abundance of great ideas and solid advice. At first I thought Londoners were different to the Irish – they were needier and more fragile, they didn't have the harsh cover of a war-torn society – yet as time passed I got an insight into some people's lives and I realised that they had had their own wars, family wars, ethnic wars, that left them just as scarred and even more vulnerable than their Belfast neighbours. Will was bemused that everyone assumed he was Irish; he insisted he was British, and was consistently laughed at.

We settled into a small two-bedroom flat which was on the third floor of an old Victorian house. It was a dark, vacant, hollow and the landlord was a fat balding Pakistani man with gold teeth who had very little English, which we reckoned was deliberate because he didn't want to converse with us regarding general maintenance. The furnished flat consisted of a rickety double bed, with a mattress that stank of stale piss, a picnic table with matching picnic chairs and an fine old chest of drawers that we later discovered had woodworm. It was depressing, but closer to the hospital that I worked in and easier to get to when the baby decided to come. Several pots of white paint transformed the floors and walls and a few geraniums and pictures reflected us as a couple in their late twenties starting afresh. Will was fussy about where things were placed; he was a bit of a perfectionist. I had to make a conscious effort not to drop my belongings at my feet when getting dressed; he provided a chair we had salvaged from a skip for my clothes in the bedroom and put up shelves for our books and photos. A black and white picture of him and his brother Sam took prominence on the shelf facing the sofa, from where we watched television. It was a reminder of why we were here. Sam was missed. We spent Saturdays trawling through markets for cheap bargains and love kept us fuelled.

I went into labour on the tube on a Monday evening after work; I was two weeks early. I tried to assure myself that it was Braxton Hicks but I knew it was more than that. I was lost amongst strange faces. I changed stations and got my final tube for home; I phoned Will to alert him, he pretended to be calm and offered to meet me at the station. The contractions started coming every ten minutes, I was frightened. I closed my eyes and imagined Nana beside me. Then I saw Sr. Nuala, I could almost hear her, smell her, see the little convent room. I saw the midwife, his face, the door that swung closed. A sharp contraction gripped my insides and caused me to let out a yelp; no-one seemed to notice. It occurred to me I could be lying on the ground giving birth and no-one would take any notice. The train stopped abruptly and the doors flew open and more commuters boarded the already overcrowded carriage. I searched for the little relics at the bottom of my bag and I held on to them. I prayed to Mary, asking for calm; it worked, the pains eased. People scanned newspapers and sat with headphones on to block out the noise. I closed my eyes again. All I could see was his little face. I opened my eyes and looked across at an old lady dressed to kill in a red velvet tight dress that clung to her skinny frame, and a white fur shawl covering her shoulders. She was wearing black patent stiletto heels. She must have been at least eighty and she smiled over at me and put a finger up to her heavily painted ruby red lips; she knew I was in labour. She put her fingers up to her eyes and closed them as if instructing me to do the same. I followed her instruction and I imagined I was sitting by a calm river, breathing steadily and listening to the wind. Only six more stops. The train stopped gently, then moved again. Only five more stops. A calmness overcame me and then a wash of warm liquid from between my legs spilled out onto the floor of the carriage. I looked over at the old lady and she was gone. A tall handsome man who was sitting next to me jumped up with a fright and walked away. I put my coat, which thankfully I had taken off, over my knees. Suddenly a blind man walked into the carriage shouting; he started to tell us his story, something about being robbed, and living homeless. He had fled his burnt-out Bosnian home, had lost his family, all of them. 'My two little girls dead, dead.' No-one was listening, they had heard it all before and didn't believe him, and they stared into nowhere eagerly contemplating their hard-earned warm dinners washed down with a cold crisp white Chardonnay. I had been one of these people so many times before tonight but tonight I heard this man and I listened to his story. He approached me with an empty woollen hat and I delved into my pockets and found a five pound note and placed it in the hat. He kissed his fingers with the five pound note and touched the holy medal that hung around his neck.

I got off at my stop and walked out into the fresh air. Will was standing there, a still, white man in shining armour, with a fresh coat and blanket. He continued to pretend to remain calm but he had parked the car on a double yellow with the back wheels on the kerb and started mumbling about going to a shop to buy nappies. He was excited and terrified because this was new to him and yet he knew but he couldn't say. Finally we got to the hospital. The labour pains came every five minutes, and they brought me straight into the delivery ward. It was when I saw the midwife put the new blue cotton baby grow and vest over the radiator that I realised this was actually happening. I did everything I was supposed to, and so did Will. We had it all planned out – a natural birth, music, candles, and a birthing ball – but nothing went to plan. I had three epidural top-ups and several shots of pethidene and still no baby, then I heard whispers of a C-section. I knew he wasn't going to survive. I knew that fear had gripped me but I couldn't let it go. I felt so alone. I just wanted Nana. The harder Will tried, the more I resented him even being there. The past had come to haunt me. I sent Will off to buy coffee, and I cried as soon as he closed the door. The monitor attached to my stomach started to beep and a midwife came in. She handed me a box of tissues.

'It will be fine,' she assured me. 'I spoke with the doctor and you are next on the list for a C-section, it should be no more than an hour.'

Will returned exhausted-looking, his brown hair and sallow skin a pale grey. I hugged him and he leaned down into my ear and whispered, 'Ella, no-one is going to take him away.'

Two hours later via a C-section a baby arrived. He had a shock of jet brown hair and wandering eyes that said I've been here before. Will held his son, and cradled him close to his chest.

He pulled a chair up beside me and showed me his little face and I started to cry again. He gently placed him in my arms and his little face looked up at me. 'I think we should call him Sam,' I said. Will nodded a yes, unable to speak.

We left the hospital the following morning. The sky was a cloak of pale, nameless grey, the wind against us and our feet a little less sure as we made it to the car with our little bundle of hope.

FOXTAILS AND SOUP

SHEILA ARMSTRONG

Have you ever heard a red fox cry, deep in the night? It is something unearthly. In days gone past, in the places between county lines that have no names, or many names, they took it for the cry of that herald of death, the banshee, and locked their doors and prayed all night for deliverance. When I was very young, I would picture them, huddled in front of a turf fire, clawing the rosary from their throats, prayer by prayer. I would snigger at their superstitions, and turn my electric blanket to full and feel safe in the aureole of red-tinted light that crept in from leftover Christmas decorations in the hallway.

But I know better now, and have often whispered clunky, half-formed prayers under my breath as the cry came bounding down the hills and through the valleys, stopping short at our house, and howling again, furious at our intrusion. It is not unlike the scream of a severed hand, or the keening of a mother who has left a child alone in the bath too long. It is a shriek, if ever there was a shriek; guttural and alive. It will freeze your marrow and you become fixated by the vacuum of silence that follows; eardrums throbbing with anticipation. Unable to move or breathe. And, worst, the cry comes out of the dark. It is terror.

When we heard the cry, we knew it was no banshee, but it would bring death all the same. We would wake, halfway, drift blearily just below the surface, and the sound would blend seamlessly with our nightmares; intangible dreams of dark, heavy things that slurped and weighed down our chests until we drowned and then awoke. When we had washed our faces of sleep, slapping and poking and pinching, and opened the back door, we knew we would find bloody feathers strewn across the field and there would be no eggs for breakfast.

But under the glaring sun, we would go hunting with our stick-swords and stick-arrows to find him. We marched and shouted and sounded our stick-horns. No bush or earth was safe from us. We would find the fox's den, and tear it apart, and stamp on his tail, and poke at his nose, and chase him with rocks. Once, we even wandered down to the sea shore, but all we found there was a huge speckled crab with one claw, a handful of cockles that we split on the rocks, and a rusted old fridge that we played in for an hour or two. It was a time machine for the afternoon, and we fought creaking and oil-slick robots who had come to take over the world.

But during the night, when the cry sounded, the cattle would spook and try to run somewhere, anywhere. They would charge at the hated electric fences, always alive with a spat-spattering of voltage, a thrum sounding every ten heartbeats, oblivious to the whip-crack shocks. Once, a mottled cow broke its leg on a twisting rock and bellowed its agony until morning. My father shot it at dawn. Another time, a young calf tried to escape through the barbed wire by the shore and managed to slit its own throat. The blood was dark and thick and the crows had already eaten out its eyes by the time we found it.

The worst were the lambs. I would cry, because I would name each and every lamb that was born to us, and knew them all well. I would tend them if their mother rejected them, closely guarding the job of feeding. I would take pleasure in each slurping gulp the lamb took from the bottle. I would follow its path down the throat, feeling the swell and contraction of the muscles, and make soft rumbling noises that came up from my belly to let the lamb know it was safe and good and well. And then I would find one mauled in the field, wool clotted with dirt and blood.

My grandmother had a fox-fur collar. I hated it; the paws were still intact and hung limply around her neck. She only wore it on important days. Once, when she had taken it in for some minor stitching, she was ambushed by protesters brandishing leaflets and T-shirts and slogans, called a murderer and a heartless bitch. Fur-is-murder, fur-is-murder.

My father set out poisoned chunks of meat for the fox and nailed shut every gap and tear in the fence, but it was no use. All we found was a couple of dead rats and, once, the sheepdog foaming and convulsing beside a lump of half-eaten meat.

So it was. The red fox gave tongue to death for all the small things of this world.

When the frost came and the too-early lambs died in frozen huddles, my father assured us that the fox had frozen too. We would cheer, imagining our foe stiff and cold under some overlooked bush. But a part of me always remained uneasy. A village is never still, you see.

Things go missing, go clunk in the night. Tractors meet on narrow roads and after-you and after-you endlessly. New jeeps are envied, planning permission signs noticed and filed away. Things go missing; or are found anew.

So I worried. Who could we fight, with our stick-swords and stick-arrows, if not the fox? Who could we blame for the stolen eggs, the broken fences, the missing calves? Our sloshing, half-filled pockets, the holes in our left boot? The hike in the bus fare, the weather, the state of the country? The fields around us would seem to loom and press closer, and those around us who had seemed so kind and twinkling under the sun became lost to us again. The Walshes; the Cannings; Mister Foley; the lady-whose-name-rhymed-with-fucker; the Healys who owned the shop; the man in the garage who let us fill our balloons from his pump; the school teacher and her friend that was more than a friend; the other children, the locals and the few whose families had trickled in searching for that elusive bucolic, probiotic lifestyle; the elusive parish priest and his nun, although we were not to say *his* nun, for she was married to Christ, or so we were told in school. It was as if some coldness in the heart would rise up, bitter and proud. But mostly, people went along with their lives, leaving behind their own little wakes that connected and merged and sometimes splashed, then calmed again.

But there was one grudge, an ancient one, that would fester even in the heat of the summer, and rise up angrily again in winter. For generations, the farm next door had been both our closest neighbours and our greatest rivals. Our grandfathers had fought, and our great-great-grandfathers had bickered, and we were no different. The current neighbour was a man named Clarke who had been two years below my father in primary school. He had had his trees cut down to stop the leaves falling on the railway lines, and was richly compensated for his supposed loss, a loss that he flaunted with a new jeep every two years and a stupid peaked cap that he imagined looked quite jaunty.

Arguments would swell and soften over the years, swell and soften, and sometimes burst like a ripe old boil. The fox got our chickens, and the neighbour somehow gained more eggs. We took a lamb or three from his fields in the night, and suckled them from bottles in the furthest corner of the barn. Once, my father's prize bull got loose and impregnated three of our neighbour's cows. Clarke said the gate had come loose, but my father was sure that it had been opened on purpose in the night. They fought for months, but my father managed to get the legal rights to any male calves born, so there was a form of peace, for a while longer. But it always lurked, in snide comments and aborted gestures.

And so it was that the worst of winter was a time of suspicion, a time to watch the neighbours from a curtained window, to count their herd, to count ours, to check the grain bins every day. Winter, when misdelivered post was left for weeks instead of being sent over to the next house by noon. A time to leave a lit lamp in the barn all night and turn on the one, solitary sensor light that hung from the awnings.

But come the melt, and the time for green things, the smiles and the handshakes returned. How-i-ya, how's-the-family, the-car, the-mortgage. And the suspicions and squinted eyes were put away for a season. Glasses were clinked. All the little grievances were still tallied, but to meet over a fence and share stories of lost lambs, or hens, and that damn-cunting-fox, was to lance the wound, if only for a while. The access rights to the lower fields would be let go, and vague threats of legal action would subside. When there could be meetings in the street that were cordial enough to avoid harsh words from spilling over, foaming on the pavement and eating away at the tarmac.

Winter was a time for war, for thinking thoughts that thickened and slurped at the sides of the head, for adding up, debiting and crediting little slights and victories. And so it was. It was an unspoken agreement.

And one January, when Clarke, in his new leather boots, dared to blame the fox for our missing chickens, my father took up his wood-axe and lodged it in his throat. My mother saw it happen from the kitchen window. She screamed, a little, and clapped her hands to her mouth and stood there, panting. She was a solid woman, not prone to flights of fancy or foolishness. Thick, in waist and mind, not like a stone, but like a swamp. We ran to the window to see what had startled her so.

And saw our father, frozen still, and the neighbour, slumped against the fence, looking ridiculous with a wooden shaft sticking out at an impossible angle from his neck. It was dusk, and swiftly growing dark, but when my father looked up, we all saw the flashing anger in his eyes which meant *we were interfering*. He gave us the same look when we were sent to fetch him from the pub, or when we tugged at his coat asking for penny sweets while he talked to the priest after mass.

My mother pulled the curtains closed. She went back to her range and stirred the stock so hard it spilled and hissed on the hot surface. She set us to chopping vegetables. I was in charge of the carrots; I liked to cut them a certain way and I would fuss and fret if one of my siblings was given the job. We worked in silence.

When the soup was done and simmering, my mother did not call my father in for supper, as she usually did. Instead we sat around the table and ate without him. She had set him a place, though, and his favourite chair seemed so wrong without him that we kept stealing glances at it to make sure he truly wasn't there. The soup was burnt, that night. I remember. My carrots were perfect, but the rest had cooked too long. No one complained.

When my father came in, much later, we were in bed, having gone without arguing this once. Our house was thin and creaky, and our rooms sat on top of the kitchen. The heat from the range wafted up and kept us warm at night, and the smell of eggs and fried bread would wake us on a Sunday morning. That night, after he came in through the back kitchen door, all we could smell was whiskey, strong and earthy.

We saw no more of our neighbour, and spoke even less of him.

And so it was that the red fox was the death of more than just small things. All things died, and all for a cry in the night.

HOUSEWIFE OF THE YEAR

ELEANOR O'REILLY

The kitchen is dark, the gloom punctuated only by the changing light caressing the window over the sink, as it swallows a lovely June evening. John Paul on his clock on the wall tick-tocks even when time should not be counted. Outside boys play, girls plan. The church bells, two streets away, knell the day to an end.

Lights. Camera. Action.

Enter Maisie Keogh, back from Confession; resplendent with telling twinkle in her eye, menopausic flush upon her cheek and three day-old mucus up her nose. She has oestrogen for the sweats; she has Panadol for the snots; she has rub for the resplendence; she wants to keep the twinkle though and she thinks she knows just how to do so.

Close-up. She puts water in the kettle. She contemplates the demise of her Jackie – termination with a lump hammer and the intention to make it look accidental. For almost as long as she's known him she's wanted to kill him. She renounces the sugar; having given it up for Lent, she no longer tolerates the warm, sweet aftertaste. One of them has to go. A good drop of milk though. It isn't going to be her.

In *flash back* episodes she revisits her life ... *A Monday ... about two years ago.*

Extreme Close-up.

Jackie's big fat head fills the frame. He is drunk and unconscious, propped against the shed, that he uses for nothing, marinating himself in a stupor of dribble, piss, vomit and lies. Even the dog looks appalled. Not surprised. Just appalled.

Voice-over begins – it's the voice of Maisie (cast as the long-suffering wife).

'Here lies Jackie Keogh. Loving Husband and Stoic Alcoholic. 1931 – 1983.

At ten o'clock this morning he went for a quick one which swiftly became seven that mysteriously mutated into a few pints for lunch, a chaser for dessert and a few sociable shorts once the mourners arrived. His mission here on earth is to drive me to kill him. My Jackie is a drinker of the hedonic variety; he drinks when he's hungry. He drinks when he's bored. He drinks when he's in company. He drinks when he's alone. He drinks when faced with feelings of deprivation or withdrawal or disappointment; when tired, unmotivated, fearful, amorous, anxious, benevolent, envious or proud. He drinks when he's happy. He drinks when he's sad. He drinks in depression and when he gets mad. In fact my Jackie tends to mistake the entire spectrum of emotions for thirst with a brain that is adept at convincing him that he is parched in almost all situations. With such insatiable cravings he is compelled on a daily basis to seek out social imperatives that normal people dread – a serial funeral-goer, this stalwart presents himself for duty whenever The Reaper gallops by. He salivates his way through the obituaries rubbing his immense idle hands in glee when a death allows him claim obligatory attendance at wake, removal and burial – an intoxicating ungodly trinity of beer, whiskey and idolatry. May he Rest in Peace.'

Fade out.

A complicated Dissolve brings Maisie and a lock shot of the tea back into view. The light source, now moved to the front, throws all else into atmospheric shadow. She sits in profile, convinced she looks slimmer that way.

Maisie considers the biscuits. Maisie considers the weight. Maisie opens the biscuits. Maisie ignores her weight by simply closing her legs to catch the belly that is most comfortable nestled there snugly between her wobbly old thighs. 'Must be the HRT,' Maisie muses. 'Can't be the biscuits,' Maisie concludes. 'And I'm certainly not going to have a baby,' Maisie predicts.

Take away one chance,
The story changes forever,
Like diamonds.

She'll never forget the first time they met (though she tries very hard) – fifty-two million Bourbon Creams, seven extra stones and twenty-six years, separating the then from the now, ease the pain of remembrance. She roots through her bag:

Sugar sachets from The Pantry – Check.

Tweezers from O'Dea's – Check.

Begonias from that ICA bitch next door – Check.

Candles from the church – Check.

Lump hammer from Flynn's haberdashery cum hardware cum

grocery – Check.

Bic biro from Bingo – Check.

With her swag all tallied up, her kleptomania satiated, her biscuit all soggy and her belly relocated she thinks back to that day when she first caught Jackie's eye.

Cue middle distance and low-budget reverberation of Beethoven's 6th:

She can see herself slipping pickled onions into her skirt. It always happens the same way; the flighty shop assistant's ridiculous blind trust teasing, daring, provoking her. She can't stand the taste of pickles. Jackie, up from the country to work in the mill, spots the beautiful blonde bandit placing her plunder in her pocket. She smiles and he's smitten.

During the first years of marriage, sexually, things (a bit like her Jackie), were simple. Lovemaking was pleasurable but (a bit like her Jackie) uninspiring, unvarying, lacklustre. Every night she would produce a new jar of ill-gotten pickles and every night her Jackie would be overcome by desire. That Little Chef pot was all that was needed in terms of an aphrodisiac and it was for her Jackie the singular erotic emblem of his early married life. The pickles made her seem more exotic, more exciting, more elusive, less likely to actually just be his Maisie. But as the years passed, a weekly jar of the forbidden fruit would do; then a monthly one was sufficient which subsequently became a bi-monthly treat, giving way later to one every trimester, and then an annual sense of duty became preserved in obligation along with the pickles until eventually the pickles produced more heartburn than hard-on.

There was always a reason not to 'do it' – a headache, a backache, a toothache, a wart.

There was always something more urgent to do – a snack, a scratch, a snooze, a snifter.

There was always a 'Not tonight, Love' that superseded a 'Sure why not, Love.'

It's Wednesday today, the midweek day of St Joseph. Tick. It was Tuesday before this and the day of the Apostles. Tock. It will be Thursday tomorrow, the day of the Blessed Sacrament. Tick. Maisie often feels crazy just counting the days as the Holy Trinity Sunday of each week just becomes the Holy Angels Monday of each week and the Blessed Virgin and her Immaculate Heart Saturday of each week follows the Christ's Passion and his Sacred Heart Friday of each week. Tick. Tock. Tick. Tock. And each week becomes each month – Tick – and each month becomes each year – Tock – and each year Maisie feels just that little bit lonelier than she did the year before. And John Paul on his clock on the wall tick-tocks even when time cannot be counted.

She gets up from the table. She rifles the press. She finds the potted pickles hiding away at the back. Tenderly she takes out the jar. Turning it upside down she reads 'Best Before Dec, '78' – that was seven years ago – before smallpox was officially eradicated from the world – so the last time they'd made love smallpox was still claiming new victims. Now the pickles (a bit like her Jackie) are embalmed in a putrid foetor of monotony, sweat and decay! They beg her in their wordless way to do something, to say something, to open the lid and take the lump hammer to them! She tosses the suicidal pickles into the bin to the scandalised applause of the voyeur inside in her own head and goes back to her storyboard.

Gentle Fade in ... from the darkness of her kitchen she is transported back to last summer – May 1984 – Thirteen months ago – about lunchtime:

Soft focus: Maisie waddles out to his shed that he uses for nothing. She's been propagating begonias from leaf cuttings she swiped from that ex-ICA bitch, with the double D cup, next door. That buxom bitch Betty Byrne, with the perfect recipe for baked alaska that Maisie will never be able to make and with all the perfect children that Maisie will never be able to have. That's how it appears to Maisie ... but the truth is that to date big busty Betty Byrne has successfully produced a failed writer and poet (still on the dole), a failed priest (still barred from the Vatican), two failed heterosexuals – one female, one male (still swapping clothes and working for the full inclusion of Lesbian, Gay, Bisexual and Transgender persons within the Youth Club up the road), a failed Irish Dancer (still in the cast) and a failed car thief (still in the Joy).

From the time hers were children, every bronze medal, every highly commended certificate, every yellow rosette, every second or third place was published in the local newspaper or announced at

Sunday mass or written in black pen across the back of the gents in the pub on the corner.

Predictably and systematically they had failed fantastically at every undertaking she had beaten and forced them to undertake. They had not failed because they had not tried. They had not failed because they had not been successful. They had failed because they were individually and indeed collectively just terrifically and terminally unintelligent but too stupid to know. Of course because of her endeavours to elevate and exalt, to immortalise and mythologise her decidedly unremarkable little gang, making each one famous for absolutely nothing, well everybody heard and everybody knew of the latest fiasco in house number two! The neighbours, as neighbours will do, wallowed joyously, relishing every failure they managed to achieve, every last place they managed to accrue. But Betty Byrne still loves her children, adoring and worshipping each one of them with an unwavering veneration, a resolute reverence that borders on incestuous and surpasses all forms of regular idolatry.

The truth is Maisie Keogh has produced nobody at all.

At that very moment Maisie can hear Betty Byrne watering the flowers in the hanging baskets outside her front porch. Betty's checking the garden that she keeps ever so neat. Although she's been blacklisted by the guild and her offspring are all mental, she still manages to make Maisie look bad. She'll not let that bitch be the only one with flower baskets flanking her front … so she mothers the begonias that she stole and won't win first place for and she forgets the children she'll not rear at all.

Tracking shot follows Maisie down the yard. Closing in on the shed, she hears movement. She stops and she listens. Pause. Inhale. She flings opens the door. Exhale. She forgets to breathe. Gasp. She sees Jackie bent over in pain. Gasp. Then the good old non verbal signals abound. Gasp – The *RTÉ Guide* – The Calor Kosangas Housewife of the Year – double page spread – all skinny and shiny. Above it stands Jackie – Gasp – all slobbery and slimy – Gasp – utilising all his stamina and wizardry, he tries to remain calm. With his penis in his hand and panic in his pants he pulls himself upright pretending that he is in fact just standing upright without his penis in his hand and without panic in his pants, in his shed, where nothing ever happens. One of them has to go. He zips up his fly. It isn't going to be her. He'll go to Hell for this. Wasn't it only this day two weeks ago that John Paul came up with a way of keeping men out of sheds? 'Masturbation, even for medical reasons, is a mortaller.' She takes comfort in that.

Fade out.

Maisie has been on her knees ever since … A novena to Margaret the Barefoot, saint of Difficult Marriages (which clearly this is); another to Dymphna, saint of Lunatics and Diabolical Possession (which would explain why Jackie is the way he is); another to Agatha of Sicily, saint of Natural Disasters (which she is hoping will kill him); another to Fiacre of Kilkenny, saint of Venereal Disease (which is really a plan B in case Agatha isn't quite up to the mark); another to Margaret of Cortona and Mary of Egypt, both saints of Prostitutes and Sexual Temptation (which is essentially to deal with the housewife and the porn in his shed); another to Joseph, saint of Doubters (which means that Maisie herself is now thoroughly struggling); another to Jude the Apostle, saint of Lost Causes (which obviously he is); and finally a novena to Andrew Avellino, saint of Sudden Death (because she'll fucking kill him quickly whenever she gets the chance!).

Establishing shot. Vertigo effect. Back in the kitchen of now, Rostropovich in unlit corner plays Prelude from Bach's Cello Suite No. 1.

Maisie lines up her tablets. A blue one – for the high blood pressure. A pink one – for the high cholesterol. Two yellows – for the diabetes. Four whites – for the osteoarthritis in her knees. A brown one – for the depression. A white one – for the hormones. A green and a gold – for the hormones. These opiates permit ingress to before … The first attack came from nowhere – the pounding, the beating, the crying – the next day saw her sore and saw her sorry – sorry she'd ever cast him in the role of husband; Jackie Keogh – a bollox of usual merit. Fantastically and reliably unreliable, extravagantly and predictably unpredictable, indolent, slothful and greedy – shamefully proud – one-dimensional like a pretend person auditioning for life – the star of his own show. One of them has to go. The smacking, the slapping, the snivelling, the swearing still seep into the script in the stern of her skull. The revulsion, the loathing, the beating – all escalating when he'd lost his job. Those were dangerous days. It isn't going to be her.

Enter Jackie Keogh, back from the pub; repulsive with purple whiskey nose, blasphemous comb-over and chain smoker's squint. Smelling of unemployment and Tayto, he wibbles and wobbles his way to his chair. One of them has to go. It isn't going to be her. One precise blow fractures his big fat head. His face caves in. His tongue hangs out. Blood oozes from both eyes and squirts out from his nose. The lump hammer is stuck in his skull. 'Oh, Jesus,' she can't get it out. She pushes. She pulls. She presses her sandal into his forehead. Her foot vanishes ankle deep, her big toe fusing with something unsavoury inside his face. She wriggles. She wiggles. She twists and she twirls but no matter how hard she tries she simply cannot successfully vacate his head. 'Fuck,' she imagines sub-titled under the scene – it's all black and white, it's all grainy and old. Then she trips over the cello secreted away in the back. 'Fucking Rostropovich. Communist Bastard,' she bellows.

Overhead shot shows Maisie prostrate among the props.

Gagging for breath, groping for release, she lies spreadeagled – is she having a heart attack? Or is it her tights? Unable to find a ladderless pair earlier, she'd resigned herself to wearing the small Pretty Pollys she'd bought back in '77 to incentivise slimming. That hadn't exactly happened – they were still far too tight. She'd improvised rather creatively, and forced her supersized legs into the thick nylons with preposterous panting and pushing; with ridiculous results she'd stretched them over legs, bum and hips with her best industrial-support knickers holding them up on the outside. Belly and gusset parted ways about noon. Knees met crotch cradle straight after lunch in an unsettling scratchy coalition of Siamese commitment – they'd been bound in that unholy union ever since. Her thighs had slapped together all afternoon, being coerced into chafing by the fat, the knees and that wayward crotch seam. After a minute or so she heaves her massive bulk forwards, then back, lots of panting, more sweating, eventually manoeuvring herself on to her side. She stares into the face of her Jackie.

Maisie brings up the credits of her own cinematic history.

Drunken useless husband … Jackie.

Director … Jackie.

First Assistant Director … Jackie.

Second Assistant Director … Jackie.

Producer … Jackie.

Executive Producer … Jackie.

Location Manager … Jackie.

Production Sound Mixer ... Jackie.

Casting Director … Jackie.

Screenwriter … Jackie

Wardrobe … Maisie.

Hair and Make-up … Maisie.

Editor … Maisie.

Cinematography … Maisie.

Maisie has seen this home movie too many times. Intermission.

She thinks she hears music – organ music – Bach in D minor – the toccata bit. Or is that the sound emanating from this noisy new corpse? Death doesn't seem to stop her Jackie doing all the things he excels at – then again, the things he excels at are all pretty basic. He pisses himself then he shits in his pants. He twitches. He moans. He groans. He sprawls in his own curry chips and dead stinking farts. 'Christ, I've never seen you more active,' she exclaims. And then comes his triumphalist last gesture, his fait accompli, his final two fingers, as the recalcitrant Jackie cadaver achieves only in death the erection he's been avoiding for years. 'You bollox,' she shrieks as he ejaculates his final goodbye. 'Bless me, Father, for I have sinned …'

Wishing her farewell

Begonias flop exhausted

On summer footpaths.

Eye twinkle fades and is gone.

And John Paul on his clock on the wall tick-tocks even when time no longer needs to be counted.

THE CROWN OF SNOW

ANNE MACDONALD

Athick veil of ice particles hung heavily in the air leaving the cathedral trees a white impression of shiny glass windows. Around the side of the ranch house, a grove of birch trees shape themselves into cathedral windows. When the trees are bare, white to the bone, they become pointed cathedral windows. From the attic, the cathedral trees gave view to the crown of snow; a range of craggy peaks shooting 14,000 feet into Colorado's thin North Park atmosphere.

Grandfather wandered from the ranch house, across the junk-filled yard to the shed on the far side of the dirt road. Bundled against the cold in a fur-lined jacket and baggie jeans, his slow walk and the fading of his figure into the ice fog gave the sense of a massive prehistoric being wandering lost within the image of a world.

Uncle Larry entered Kate's attic room. 'Goin' into Walden, Granddaughter.' He placed a folded newspaper on the round table, and tapped three times with his middle finger – Uncle Larry's way of pointing out importance, worry or discipline. 'Watch your Grandpa today. He's thinking of things that could have been. He almost married this here woman.'

Outside, Grandfather squinted blindly into the ice fog, through the cathedral trees and up to the crown of snow. He turned in a floating motion from the icy stillness around him, shook himself several times, puttered about the junk yard, wiped his feet and stood at the entrance of the old shed. Larry tapped three more times, pointed to the obituary, and left.

The photograph showed an old woman with grey curly hair. The woman's eyes were clear, bright and young. The old woman had lived a real life, not the life within a dream, a plan, a hope. Grandfather's eyes were never young. At eighty-five, he looked a hundred and five. In his sixties, he looked eighty-five. That's when Kate came to live with him. Her parents had frozen to death on a remote road near the Alkali Butte in Wyoming. She had been staying with Grandfather and Uncle Larry on that day, and so simply remained. The ranch house became her life; the crown of snow her backdrop.

Kate banged on the attic window and motioned Grandfather to wait. She climbed down the stairs, grabbed Uncle Larry's ranch coat, and left the house, working her way through the discarded engines, tractor parts, mufflers, bits and pieces of failed chicken coops and fencing, joining Grandfather near the shed.

He motioned to the crown of snow, barely visible through the melting ice particles. 'Can't touch that, Granddaughter. Can't get near it. Can't grab it, can't be a part of it, can't take it to your being, can't hold it, touch it, can't make it part of your soul. All you can do is look at it, let its beauty and wonder run a quick thrill through you, and let it go. Spirit and mind? Those are just words with no meaning. If there was such a thing as spirit, if mind was more than our brain connections, we'd feel that thrill of wonder forever. That wonder would turn into harmony, and spirit would be a word with meaning.'

Not many people could communicate with Grandfather, except Uncle Larry, and within a few years of living with them, Kate. By the time she was of the age to understand such things, she knew why the ranch was a neglected centre of long-forgotten and hopeless dreams, and why the Irish ancestor had split from the twelve other wagons and settled on an expanse of land that showed no possibility for ranching success, accepting social isolation and economic failure as the price for independent spiritual searching at the foot of the crown of snow; that a perpetual yearning to understand, to grasp and hope that the surrounding beauty of nature would lead to a harmony. But, of course, it never would. There would only be the journey with no spiritual guide, no ancient *fili*, for the ancestor, no seer for Grandfather or for Uncle Larry.

Ice fog lingered around the aspens and ponderosa pines. Muffled voices rose from the glens. Small, shabby otherworldly figures moved about and through the frost-covered trees and bushes.

'The Hooligans are out,' Grandfather noted as he wiped his feet and entered the broken-down shed. 'Keep them away from the house.'

The neighbour ranch kids, aptly named *Hoolihan*, slithered and crawled towards the house, eight or nine of them. Their games periodically led to daring raids on Grandfather's food storage and kitchen areas.

Kate gave chase to the Hooligans, herding them from the kitchen, through the living room and out the front door. The littlest ones scurried like chickens, food in their mouths, drink in their hands. The pushing, herding and shoving was loud and chaotic. Each time she got one out the front door, another would sneak past, run back into the house, raid the cupboards. When she counted the last one out and watched them graze about in the junkyard, she turned.

At the back door stood the oldest of the tribe, eighteen-year-old Mickey. 'Didn't mean to scare you, Katie. I'm here to see about work.'

Outside, the other Hooligans looked like contented cows among the junk in the yard.

'No one works much around here.' She motioned to Grandfather in the shed. 'He's in a mood today, but you can try.'

By eight o'clock that night, Mickey had cleaned the junkyard, bedded the horses, propped the shed. Larry was back from whatever Larry did once a week in Walden, and Grandfather, Larry, Mickey and Kate sat down to supper. The pall of busyness and work huddled about them. No one mentioned the lady in the newspaper.

When the others had gone to bed, Grandfather eased himself into the chair near the fireplace. 'Best get to college somewhere, Katie,' he said. 'Not that it matters much. But if you need to keep yourself busy and don't want to spend your life wishing to understand a mountain, peaks of snow and birch trees that form themselves into matter, might as well go to college. You don't want to live a life where the fantasy becomes your reality.'

'Like the dead woman in the newspaper? You were going to marry her. Larry told me …'

'She was a world's creature – that side of humanity that busies itself with living. The type that finds happiness and wonderment and fulfilment through what other humans think; existing on the admiration, envy and desires of others; living well and happily by entering others' limited space and time. We're not like that, Granddaughter. We're among the humans who live a private existence. We experience occasional happiness. When I look through those trees on an icy morning, or the snow peaks on a summer's day, that's all I need, because that's all there is, and even that doesn't really matter. We have a tremor of harmony on a periodic basis, and wait patiently for the next. Might as well not hope for more. We don't enter anyone else's existence. If they want us, they come to us and enter our world. Like Mickey there; he's come to enter your existence. But move on, girl. Head for glory, not just that which is in your head.' Grandfather sat quietly for the next few minutes, arms resting on the easy chair, his eyes firm on the fire. He motioned out the dark window, through the cathedral trees, and towards the craggy crown of snow. 'Bury me up there, Granddaughter.'

In late spring, Larry, Mickey and Kate climbed past timberline. They crawled about steep, broken crags and lichen-covered rocks. They hiked through early summer alpine brooks. Tremors of peace and beauty and harmony came and went, leaving in their wake the ancestral longing to blend into the splendour of the deep blue sky, the white craggy crown of snow, the gray rock peaks, the alpine streams.

'Can't have any of this.' Uncle Larry waved it away. 'That's the trouble with it all. Can't have a beautiful painting, can't hear the wonder of song, can't feel the touch of poetry without wanting it forever. Can't grasp it to your being. Can't be a part of its existence. The quick orgasm of harmony can't last forever. In the end, spirit and mind are only words for something a human needs, but can't never have. The beauty always ends.' He stopped, pulled the bottle from his pack, took a swig. 'I have trouble with that,' he finally said.

They found a spot within the glacial arms of the crown of snow, as high up as they could go and still transport, in some manner or form, illegally as hell, the frozen body of Grandfather. Several ground-level, wind-torn cedars surrounded the spot, and an alpine brook trickled near. The grave would be between two quartz rocks, each of which glimmered from the wind, snow and weather that had smoothed it to a finished shine.

Uncle Larry tapped the one rock three times with his middle finger and looked over the area. 'Yep.' He tapped again. 'This is the spot.'

The three of them dug through the mud, the dirt, and broke up the deep ice.

Days later, Uncle Larry, Kate, Mickey and four other Hooligans loaded the pine box onto the old Ford pickup and banged and bounced up the dirt road. When the Ford got stuck in icy mud, they pulled the pine-box coffin from the pickup, placed it on a small wagon and pushed, pulled and lifted it up the deer trail and into the glacial bowl.

By the time the sun disappeared behind the peaks and the thin mountain air turned cold, Grandfather was in the hole. The Hooligans ran wild among the alpine tundra. Uncle Larry picked up the bottle of whiskey they had transported in the coffin. 'I want my body up here too.' He toasted Grandfather, took a swig and passed the bottle to Mickey.

Mickey held the bottle to the air. 'To Grandfather.' Just that day, Mickey had driven into Walden and joined the Marines.

Katie took a swig, but she had no toast to Grandfather. Harmless meanderings of the mind, coasting wills of the spirit, clear, clean streams of relaxed madness that trickled from her ancestral pool; she would leave those behind.

BIOGRAPHIES

Sheila Armstrong grew up in Sligo and attended college in Dublin. She is a freelance editor and is working on a short story collection.

Eithne Cavanagh's work has been published widely in journals and anthologies. Her poetry has received awards including the Boyle Poetry Prize and the Moore Gold Medallion. She facilitates creative writing courses. Two collections of her poetry, *Bone and Petal,* and *An Elegance of Gannets,* have been published by Swan Press.

Robert Grossmith has had a novel published by Hamish Hamilton and a number of published stories, several of them reprinted in the *Best Short Stories* series and *The Penguin Book of First World War Stories.* He works as a dictionary editor.

Bill Hoagland's poetry has appeared in *The Denver Quarterly, Gray's Sporting Journal, Nebraska Review, Poem, Seneca Review, Writers' Forum, South Coast Poetry Journal,* and many other journals, as well as in the anthologies *The Last Best Place* and *Ring of Fire: Writers of the Yellowstone Region.* He published a chapbook of poems entitled *Place of Disappearance,* and was the recipient of two Wyoming Arts Council awards in creative writing – a Fellowship in Creative Writing and a Neltje Blanchan Nature Writing Award. He holds an MFA from the University of Massachusetts and taught creative writing and other courses at Northwest College in Powell, Wyoming, until his retirement in 2013. Originally from Illinois, today he lives in Cork, Ireland.

Anne MacDonald's fiction includes a novel, *A Short Time in Luxembourg* (Milwaukee: Gardena Press, 2004), and short stories published in *Dublin Quarterly, Blue Earth Review, Matter: the Journal of Art and Literature. Tales of Thirst and Longing* (fiction anthology) and the *Bellestrist Review*. She holds a BA in History from UC Berkeley; an MA in History from Colorado State University; an MLS from University of Washington, Seattle, and a Diploma in Irish Studies from National University of Ireland, Galway.

Karen J. McDonnell's fiction, non-fiction, travel writing and poetry have been published in *Crannóg*, *poeticdiversity* (in Los Angeles), *SIN*, *The Clare Champion*, *The Irish Times* and by the Clare Poets Group, of which she is a member. She was a featured poet at the 2013 Strokestown Poetry Festival. Her poem *Aubade*, which prefaces a poetic song-cycle *Notes from the Margins*, won the NUI Galway poetry competition.

Aoife Mannix was born in Sweden of Irish parents. She grew up in Dublin, Ottawa and New York before moving to the UK. She is the author of four collections of poetry and a novel, *Heritage of Secrets*. She has been poet in residence for the Royal Shakespeare Company and BBC Radio 4's *Saturday Live*.

Susan Millar DuMars has published three poetry collections with Salmon Poetry, the most recent of which, *The God Thing*, appeared in March, 2013. She also published a book of short stories, *Lights in the Distance*, with Doire Press in 2010. Her work has appeared in publications in the US and Europe and in several anthologies, including *The Best of Irish Poetry 2010*. She has read from her work in the US, Europe and Australia. Born in Philadelphia, Susan lives in Galway, Ireland, where she and her husband Kevin Higgins have coordinated the Over the Edge readings series since 2003.

Siobhan Murtagh received an honourable mention from New Millennium Writings Awards 33. She was highly commended in the Sean O'Faolain International Short Story Competition, 2013 and shortlisted in Carousel Writers' Competition.

Marcella O'Connor is currently writing a dissertation on Elizabeth Bowen at University College Cork. Her fiction has appeared or is forthcoming in *Ambit*, *Cyphers* and *Crannóg*.

Michael O'Connor lives in Ballybrack, Co. Dublin and teaches in St Nicholas Montessori College, Dún Laoghaire. He was a prizewinner in the Troubadour International Poetry Competition, 2011. He was commended in the Dromineer Poetry Competition, 2013 and he has been published in *Crannóg*, *The Stony Thursday Book*, *WOW! Anthology 2010* and elsewhere.

Orlagh O'Farrell has been published in *Cork Literary Review*, *Crannóg* and *Longford Literary Virtual Writer*. She won second prize in the Strokestown International Poetry Competition, 2008. She is a member of Airfield Writers' Group.

Eleanor O'Reilly is a teacher of English and Classical Studies. She has been shortlisted for the James Plunkett Award and the Over The Edge New Writer of the Year, both in 2013. She won the William Trevor/Elizabeth Bowen Literary Award in 2013.

Julia Roddy has worked as a writer, director, production-designer and consultant on both documentary and fiction film. She has exhibited paintings in Ireland, England and America. She has received awards with the Royal Academy of Arts and has various private collectors. She has managed the Galway film festival and consulted and facilitated short films with community groups. She currently lectures at the GMIT in screen writing and has just completed her first novel, *Orange Boy Blue*.